Ruby Rogers
Who Are You Looking At?

Ruby Rogers
Who Are You
Looking At?

Sue Limb

Illustrations by Bernice Lum

BLOOMSBURY

First published in Great Britain in 2008 by Bloomsbury Publishing Plc
36 Soho Square, London, WID 3QY

A CIP catalogue record of this book is available from the British Library

ISBN 978 0 7475 9249 5

All papers used by Bloomsbury Publishing are natural, recyclable
products made from wood grown in well-managed forests.
The manufacturing processes conform to the environmental
regulations of the country of origin.

Printed in Great Britain by Clays Ltd, St Ives Plc

1 3 5 7 9 10 8 6 4 2

www.suelimb.com
www.bloomsbury.com

CHAPTER 1
Oh my God! It's a fight!

'SO, RUBY?' Mrs Jenkins stared at me. My mind went blank. I panicked. I felt myself go red. 'Oh, never mind,' she said, as if I was some kind of idiot. 'Yasmin?'

'Miss, I want to be a fashion designer. And I'll have shows in aid of the rainforest and things.'

'Good. Anybody else? – Dan?'

'I'm going to design cars, miss, that don't emit nasty gases.' Crumbs! Froggo was such a brainbox! My friends were all so switched on, but I didn't have a clue. I was like an electric light bulb that has gone phizz-phut and turned dark and tinkly.

I racked my brains. What was I going to be? I had to think of something. Jenko would ask me again in a minute. I couldn't think of any jobs at all – except being a teacher (my dad) or a midwife (my mum). If Jenko picked on me again, I'd say I was going to be a nurse. But how would that help to stop climate change? Jenko won't be satisfied until her whole class is saving the planet.

'Leo?' said Mrs Jenkins. Leo is the new boy in our class. His first day was yesterday. He's tall (almost as tall as Max) and he's got long black hair. Some of it's slicked back and some falls across his face. He's got big brown eyes, and yesterday, when

we were doing our get-to-know-you stuff, sitting in a circle, he had a cool kind of look on his face, as if he didn't care that we were looking at him.

Leo said he wanted to be a DJ, which wasn't anything to do with the environment as far as I could see.

'How could that help the environment?' asked Jenko. Leo frowned and smoothed his hair back. 'Anybody?' she went on.

'Please, miss, Leo could tell people about recycling schemes and things!' said Froggo.

'And make appeals for money for the rainforests and stuff!' added Toby.

'Exactly!' said Jenko. 'Leo would be in a wonderful position to influence the way people think about things, to spread important ideas, wouldn't he?' Leo blushed slightly and looked a bit surprised that his choice of job had turned out to be so eco-friendly.

I felt sorry for him. It's horrible being new. I remembered when Lauren was new, nobody would speak to her for a while because she looked weird. I only looked after her because Mrs Jenkins told me to. But once I got to know her, of course, she was really nice and rewarded me with trips to her divine farm, where I cuddled lots of cute baby animals, including her small brothers and sister.

'So,' Mrs Jenkins went on. 'Who's next? – Max? Have you got any plans for your future career?'

'Miss, I want to be an architect.'

'Ah, now that's a very important line of work, isn't it? Who can tell me why?'

Max rambled on for a bit about the houses he was going to build having solar panels and stuff. We'd learned about solar panels last week, so that was easy.

Yasmin waited until Mrs Jenkins wasn't looking, and then whispered, 'Isn't Leo a *babe*?' I think she'd been impressed by the idea of him as the DJ who saved the world. I ignored her. I get a bit embarrassed when she says things like that.

It was Lauren's turn to talk about her possible future career. She wants to run a riding stable. Everybody thought this would be very good for the environment, because it would give people the chance to take exercise in the fresh air. But nobody mentioned about horses farting.

Joe told me once about cows and sheep burping and farting. Apparently it's one of the causes of global warming. And if the animals are causing all that damage, what about us? Especially my brother Joe. He set fire to his once. I laughed so much I cried. If Mrs Jenkins asked me again what I was going to do with my life, and how I would do my bit to combat climate change, I would be so tempted to say, *Please miss, I'm going to stop burping and farting.*

'Ruby? What's so funny?'

My blood froze. 'Nothing, sorry.'

'What are you smirking at? What's so amusing? We're trying to have a serious discussion.'

'Sorry, Mrs Jenkins.'

'So what are you going to do with your life, Ruby Rogers? Have you had any ideas yet?'

I panicked again. My mind went so blank for a split second I didn't even see in colours. Everything went black and white.

'Ruby's going to be a gangster!' said Froggo.

Everybody laughed – except Mrs Jenkins.

'A gangster, is it, Ruby?' she demanded, folding her arms and glaring. Sometimes I don't think she likes me *at all.*

I do have a kind of daydream that I will be a gangster. I'd live in the trees with my gang, who would be a mixture of monkeys and people, and we'd rob the rich and give the money to poor people. And poor monkeys. But it all sounded totally stupid compared to my friends' plans. They were so mature and *realistic*.

'Please, miss, I want to be a teacher!' I said. It was a total lie, of course. Mrs Jenkins gave me a bad-tempered look. She probably thought I'd only said that to suck up to her. But really I'd only said that because it was the one thing I could think of. I could never be a nurse, because I don't like the sight of blood. I don't think I'd mind so much if it was green.

'You'll have to buck your ideas up if you want to be a teacher!' said Mrs Jenkins with the hint of a sneer. 'It takes a lot of dedication and focus and

hard work, and let's face it, Ruby, you're a bit of a dreamer, aren't you?'

I nodded. She was right, actually. I am a bit of a dreamer. I dreamed last night I was a sardine.

Mrs Jenkins moved on. She'd obviously decided she wasn't going to get much more out of me. It seemed that everybody in my class was headed for what Mrs Jenkins called 'rewarding and meaningful work' – except me.

I was amazed at how everybody had been thinking about their future and making plans, while I had just been staring into space and dreaming I was a sardine.

At lunchtime Yasmin grabbed me and Hannah. She would have grabbed Lauren too if she'd had three arms.

'Listen!' she hissed. 'I've had a brilliant idea! We can form a gang and have a secret plan!'

'Sounds OK to me,' I replied. I love secret plans, in fact I try to have at least one on the go at all times.

'Oh, great!' said Lauren. 'Like the Famous Five?'

'We'll be the Fabulous Four!' whispered Yasmin. 'Are you up for it, Hannah?'

'I *so* am!' breathed Hannah. 'What's the secret plan?'

'I'll tell you the plan once we've made our solemn vow,' said Yasmin. 'Normally we'd prick our fingers and mix our blood, but as we're at school we'll have to make do with spit.'

'How?' asked Lauren, looking worried.

'We spit in one another's hands and then shake hands,' said Yasmin.

'Urghhhhh!' said Hannah. 'We'll have to do it in the cloakrooms, then, and wash our hands straight away afterwards.'

We went to the girls' loos, spat in each other's hands (screaming horribly the whole time) and then shook hands all round. Then we washed our hands.

'OK,' said Hannah. 'So now we're the Fabulous Four, what's the secret plan?'

'We're going to capture Leo,' said Yasmin proudly, as if it was a brilliant idea instead of a load of complete twaddle.

'Capture?' Lauren looked worried again. 'What do you mean? *Kidnap?*' She wrinkled her nose.

'Not *kidnap*, you muppet!' said Yasmin, laughing. 'I mean, make sure he's our best friend. Make him adore us. Make him think we're the coolest people on the planet. Make him, like, totally *in lurve* with us!'

Hannah jumped up and down and clapped her hands. 'Yessss!' she said. Lauren raised her eyebrows and gave a nervous little smile. My heart sank. If I'd known how stupid Yasmin's secret plan was going to be, I'd never have joined the gang in the first place.

But what could I do? If I told her what I thought, she'd only get in a strop and have a massive row. Yasmin can sulk for days if necessary. In a couple of days it was going to be our school trip. And we just had to be friends for that – otherwise it would be ruined.

So although I felt really annoyed about it, I tagged along when a gang of us gathered around Leo, to be friendly, or (in Yasmin's case) to launch her secret plan to sweep him off his feet and make him her own for ever.

He wasn't really shy – far from it.

'Your teacher is, like, an alien,' he said with a sly grin.

'You're so right!' yelled Yasmin. 'I always thought there was something weird about her! I love aliens! Which are your favourites?'

I love Yasmin, but I don't like it when she goes a bit over the top and tries to impress people. Everybody started swapping alien stories until the bell went for afternoon school. The louder Yasmin got, the more silent I became. But I quite like being silent. Even if some people do think I'm a loser compared to her.

However, I'm not a total loser, because I have a teenage friend, glamorous goth legend Holly Helvellyn, and she walked home with me after school. She's often passing our school at home time because she's been working in the art room of Ashcroft School. Holly's leaving at the end of this term, though, and going to art college. In fact she's sort of left already, but she keeps going back to use the art room – all the paints and stuff.

'So how was your day, Ruby?' she asked, peering at me from under the rim of a stylish sunhat. She isn't all that gothic now it's summer, actually – she's lightened up a bit. She was wearing a long white lace dress and pale make-up, which looked very dramatic with her black hair. Her hair used to be red but I like it better dark. I used to wish she and my bro Joe would get together, but I have totally given up on that now.

'My day was horrid,' I said. 'Everybody was telling Mrs Jenkins what they're planning to do when they grow up, and I couldn't think of anything, and I kind of blanked out and felt like a total nerd.'

'Never mind, Ruby!' Holly laughed. 'You can't be a worse nerd than me!'

'You're not a nerd!' I shouted. 'You're a legend!'

'Well, maybe I'm a legendary nerd,' said Holly with a grin. 'Shall we go to the Dolphin Cafe for a quick drink?'

'Great idea!' I grinned. I was feeling much better now. Holly would help me to think of a career. She is so brilliant.

I texted my mum to tell her where I was going, and then we began to plan what we'd have at the Dolphin. But when we got there, there was a nasty noise coming from inside. It was a kind of yelling and banging. Not gunfire kind of banging, more like furniture falling over. Then a couple of boys burst out of the door, pulling each other's clothes about.

'Oh my God!' said Holly. 'It's a fight. Come away, Ruby!' She grabbed my hand and ran off down the road. Once we'd turned the corner and we were safe, she stopped running. 'Toby Wallace and his stupid gang!' she sighed, shaking her head. 'They're such idiots.'

CHAPTER 2

What are you laughing at?

I T WAS DISAPPOINTING that the stupid gang had ruined our plans for tea in the Dolphin Cafe. We didn't talk much as we walked home. Holly seemed to be thinking of something else. When we got to my house I invited her in. There was a horrible noise of TV violence in the sitting room. We went in there. Joe was sprawled on the sofa and his socks smelt like a major environmental disaster.

'Hi, Rogers,' said Holly casually. 'Getting your usual violence fix?'

'It's *Gangs of New York*,' replied Joe. 'Lethal stuff.'

'Switch it off,' said Holly. 'Ruby's here.'

'Take her out if you're so bothered,' grunted Joe. There was a lot of blood and screaming on the TV, so I ran into the kitchen. Holly followed me.

'Let's have some hot chocolate,' I said. Holly looked a bit edgy.

'I don't think I can, Ruby, sorry,' she said. 'I've got to get home. Things to do.' And she went. I suppose it was something to do with Joe. He should have switched the TV off, jumped up politely and come out to have a hot chocolate with us. He's useless.

I had a hot chocolate by myself, reading the *Beano*. It was quite funny, but I noticed that nearly all the characters were boys. OK, there was Minnie, but there should be lots and lots – different sorts of girls. I mean, take our class: there's Yasmin, pushy and bossy, Lauren, shy and outdoorsy, Hannah, giggly and an airhead, and me, legendary nerd. And that's just on our table.

But what sort of girl am I? I went upstairs. Joe came out of the sitting room. (The TV was switched off now, half an hour too late.)

'Where's what's-her-name?' he called up the

stairs. He always pretends to forget Holly's name, as if he never thinks about her. Although, maybe that's the truth. Maybe he just never does. Anyway, like I said, I've given up on the whole project. Matchmaking is a mug's game.

I didn't even answer him. I just went to the bathroom and locked myself in. I stared in the mirror. Maybe it was because I'd just been reading the *Beano*, but actually, with my crazy sticking-out hair, I looked rather like a sad, serious Dennis the Menace of the female sort.

I sat on the loo and wished I wasn't of the female sort. Boys can pee standing up, for a start. I'd love to do that. I tried it once but it was a disaster. There's no need to go into gross details, but I had to have a shower straight away.

After peeing, I still hung around the bathroom. I wetted my hair and slicked it back to try to look gangsterish. But how was I ever going to make it as a gangster when I couldn't stand the sight of blood? I even get upset when somebody kills a wasp.

The laundry basket was in there and it was full to overflowing. One of Mum's bras was hanging out. I picked it up and inspected it. All those straps and hooks – what a nightmare. That would be another advantage of being a boy. You wouldn't have to wear a bra, ever.

I took off my T-shirt and tried Mum's bra on – just for a laugh. I had to tie it in a knot at the back because it was way too big. I found a pair of dad's socks and rolled them up and put them in the cups. Then I put my T-shirt on again. I looked hilarious. I literally laughed till I cried. I rolled around on the floor.

There was a knock on the door. 'How much longer are you going to be in there?' It was Joe. 'And what are you laughing at?'

'Something I read in the *Beano*!' I yelled back.

Hastily I pulled off the bra and socks, and shoved them back in the laundry basket. I put on my T-shirt again and slipped out of the bathroom into my room.

Once I was safe in my tree-house bed-platform, I talked things over with my monkeys.

'Guys,' I said, 'I don't want to grow up into a woman. I want to grow up into a monkey.'

'You can probably get an operation that would do that,' said Funky. 'But you'd have to go to California.'

'I wish I was a hippopotamus,' sighed Stinker. (He's the boss monkey and he's usually very gang-sterish.) 'But what to do? It just ain't my destiny.'

'You think you've got problems?' said Hewitt. 'I was born with a tennis racket in my hand! I can never get rid of the damn thing! It's, like, fused to my wrist! I get sick of tennis sometimes. I want to be a racing driver. How can you drive a Ferrari with a tennis racket in your hand?'

'It's probably illegal,' said Funky thoughtfully. 'Oh well. At least I can suck my own toes.' He has very bendy legs. Joe made him kiss his own bottom once. Joe is really, really gross. It was funny, though.

Next day, at break, it was raining, so we all had

to stay indoors. Leo disappeared into the boys' loos, so Yasmin and Hannah and Lauren and I went into a corner of the school hall and sat there eating Yasmin's mum's divine cheese sandwiches. We had half a sandwich each. I really like Lauren and Hannah, but there are times when I want Yasmin all to myself. Especially when there are those cheese sandwiches about.

'That Leo is a dreamboat,' said Yasmin. 'As soon as he comes in we should launch our campaign.'

'So what's our campaign going to be?' I asked.

Yasmin shrugged in an excited way.

'Anything!' She grinned. 'Tell him about aliens, make him laugh – he's got such an amazing smile, hasn't he? Ten out of ten for sex appeal! What do you think, Hannah?'

'Nine,' said Hannah.

'Froggo would only get about six,' said Yasmin. 'What about Max? Four?'

'Oh, more than four,' said Hannah. 'Max is so lovely and tall! And he's funny sometimes!' She giggled. 'Seven, maybe. Or six-and-a-half.' I was beginning to feel grumpy.

'So who's your favourite boy?' I asked Lauren. 'Or are you going to marry a horse?' Lauren looked a bit shocked, and she blushed.

'I don't know,' she said. 'I like my cousin Sam, but he lives in Manchester.'

'Look!' said Yasmin. She pulled up her sleeve to show something she'd written on her arm. It was the word LEO with a heart around it. 'When I'm sixteen I'll have some proper tattoos done,' she said.

You sooo *will not,* I thought. *Your dad would kill you!* I didn't say anything, though, because I knew it would only lead to a row.

'Don't tell Froggo I've got LEO written on my arm,' she said with a secretive giggle, 'because Leo might already have a girlfriend!'

'What's it got to do with Froggo?' asked Lauren.

'Yasmin fancies Froggo as well!' giggled Hannah. 'A bit, anyway.'

'If Leo's not available,' said Yasmin grandly, 'I'll settle for Froggo, because he's so funny. He's my Plan B.'

'And I'll settle for Max,' said Hannah. 'Because he's so tall.'

Although I didn't want to think of any boys in our class as sex gods or possible boyfriends, I did feel a bit annoyed that Yasmin had kind of assumed Froggo would be hers if she couldn't find anyone better. I was in a bad mood today, and I had a feeling it could only get worse.

CHAPTER 3
Guess what!

'I CAN'T WAIT for the school trip tomorrow!' whispered Yasmin in art. 'We must make sure we sit next to Leo! And you know my star sign is Leo – amazing coincidence, yeah? Well, guess what star sign he is?'

Hannah grinned and raised her eyebrows. She seemed to be in on the secret already.

I was so fed up of Yasmin and Hannah drooling over Leo, I decided I wouldn't cooperate with this little game.

'Uhh . . . was he born under the sign of Yasmin?' I suggested in a sarcastic voice.

'Don't be stupid, Ruby!' she snapped. She wasn't in the mood for jokes. 'I asked him what star sign he was and he said Aquarius!' I shrugged. 'Guess what!' hissed Yasmin. 'Aquarius's ideal partner is *Leo*!'

I smiled. I had to humour her. If not, she'd get in a strop and possibly stage a row. I had to wriggle out of this insane Fabulous Four rubbish with its pathetic plan to 'capture' Leo.

'I asked him what his favourite colour was and he said blue!' whispered Yasmin.

So what? He liked blue – I mean, who doesn't?

'Plus he's obsessed with aliens,' whispered Hannah. 'We should get a book out of the library all about aliens and dazzle him with our fabulous knowledge!'

'Brilliant idea!' gasped Yasmin.

I sighed. I was beginning to feel like an alien, myself. I was looking forward to the school trip tomorrow and I didn't want to get sidetracked by Yasmin banging on about Leo all the time.

Last lesson in the afternoon was history. Mrs Jenkins told us all about our visit to the castle and the arboretum. She also went on about safety for ages, which was a bit boring. She told us we must at all times obey her and the other adults who would be coming: the teaching assistant Miss Roberts (who has thin, weedy legs and mad, staring eyes), Charlie's mum and Sophie's dad.

'Never forget,' said Jenko solemnly, 'castles and woodland are dangerous places.' The main danger as far as I could see was that Yasmin and Hannah might both grab Leo and tear him in half, but Mrs Jenkins didn't mention that.

Next day when we climbed aboard the bus, Froggo, Max, Toby and Leo went straight to the back, where there was that long seat that goes all

the way across. Yasmin barged after them. Hannah followed her. I knew Yasmin would want me to sit by her and would be stressy if I didn't cooperate, so I went down to the back as well. The boys all hurled themselves on to the long seat. There was one empty seat at the end, by the window.

'I'll sit there!' said Yasmin, plonking herself down beside Froggo. She hadn't managed to sit next to Leo, but there was only Froggo between her and her Love God, and as Froggo was her Plan B, that was OK anyway. Hannah sat in one of the seats just in front, and Lauren and I in the other seat across the aisle. Suddenly Mrs Jenkins' voice boomed out.

'Dan Skinner! Max! Toby! I'm not having you boys all together at the back like that! Come up here and sit at the front where I can see you!'

Grumbling and muttering, Froggo and co got up and slouched back up to the front. Yasmin looked annoyed. She beckoned us to join her. We now had the big back seat all to ourselves, which was ace. There was one spare seat.

'Nadia, go and sit at the back next to Lauren!' said Mrs Jenkins. Oh no! Smelly Nadia. Her friend Jules with the annoying laugh was away today, so we'd have her tagging along with us. Apart from being smelly, she is disgusting in other ways. She wriggled herself in beside poor Lauren and immediately tossed some gum into her mouth without offering it round to anybody.

The teaching assistant, Miss Roberts, came and sat nearby. Sophie's dad and Charlie's mum were sitting towards the middle of the bus. Charlie's mum was incredibly pretty but Sophie's dad looked a bit like a heron. I was glad neither of my parents were available to come on the school trip. I would literally faint with embarrassment.

'Guess what!' whispered Nadia, as the bus started up and moved off. 'I'm wearin' my new bra.'

'NO!' breathed Yasmin. 'I don't believe you!' She sounded kind of impressed. I hated her for it. I just ignored Nadia and stared right ahead, into the distance, like Leo had done when he first came into our classroom.

'What d'you call this, then?' snapped Nadia, and she pulled her top up and flashed her underwear right at us. I kind of had to look even though I didn't want to. No kidding – it was a real bra, with lace and straps and everything.

Yasmin screamed. Lauren screamed. Hannah screamed. I groaned. It was partly the shock, partly envy (on Yasmin's part), partly amazement and,

in my case, surprise that Nadia would show everybody her undies on a school trip.

Our scream echoed through the bus. Miss
Roberts looked round and frowned slightly. Mrs
Jenkins jumped to her feet and came pounding
down the aisle to us, with a face like thunder.

'What's going on?' she demanded, glaring at us
one by one.

'Please, miss,' said Nadia in her husky voice,
'Ruby just told us a rude joke.'

'I did *not*!' I exploded. 'That's a lie!'

'It is a lie, Mrs Jenkins!' Yasmin added, backing
me up. 'Ruby didn't tell us a joke.'

28

'Be quiet, all of you!' said Jenko. 'Now listen. If I hear one more peep out of any of you, I'm telling the driver to turn round and we'll go back to school and drop you there. You can sit in Mrs Wakefield's office all day and do exercises. Is that clear?'

We all said, 'Yes, miss,' and looked very meek and mild and sorry, because the idea of missing the school trip was more than we could bear. I prayed that Nadia wouldn't be tagging along with us all day, because she'd already got us into trouble and we'd only been driving along for about two minutes.

I decided to ignore her. I got out my school trip schedule. It was a piece of paper Mrs Jenkins had given us after registration. It had everything we were going to do:

HISTORY YEAR 6
Trip to Fairfax Castle, forest and arboretum.

1) What was it like to live here in the past?
2) What can we learn about the environment from visiting the arboretum?
3) Why is the forest important?

10.30 a.m.	Arrive at Fairfax Castle. Tour of castle.
12.00 p.m.	Picnic lunch in Castle Grounds. (If wet, in the Barn Café.)
12.30 p.m.	Worksheets in groups.
1.30 p.m.	Visit Arboretum. Introductory talk.
2.30 p.m.	Walk in groups. Worksheets.
3.30 p.m.	Picnic teas and home.

During the visit you must complete your worksheets, and don't forget the photo competition.

Apart from the magic words 'picnic lunch' and 'picnic tea', what I was really looking forward to most was the photo competition. Joe had lent me his digital camera and I couldn't wait to point it at all those trees. Although I had a feeling that several people's cameras were going to be pointed at Nadia's bra.

CHAPTER 4
Shut up, you idiot!

S OON THE BUS left the edge of the
town and rolled through the countryside. I
stared out of the window. Lauren was reading a
book about ponies. Yasmin, Hannah and Nadia
were talking about boys all the time. How boring.
But at least Yasmin wasn't going on about her
secret plan to capture Leo, because Nadia was
there.

I started to think about a brilliant career that
would not involve anything to do with boys.
Teaching would be no good because I'd have to

teach boys – unless I taught at a girls' school. But then the girls would be giggling about boys all the time, the losers. I sighed. Maybe the problem was girls, not boys.

Maybe I *could* be a nurse, but the sort of nurse that never has to see blood. I imagined myself in an operating theatre. The surgeon was a very brilliant woman called Miss Sherwood and she had never noticed boys in her life.

Expertly she sliced through the gleaming skin of a famous footballer, avoiding his tattoo. 'Swab?' she said gruffly to me. My eyes were closed, so I couldn't see the blood. The other nurse, whose name was Mandy Willows, handed Miss Sherwood the swab.

'Isn't he a babe!' Mandy sighed, gazing down on the footballer. 'Nine out of ten for sex appeal! Would it be unprofessional to cut off a lock of his hair while he's unconscious?'

Was there no escape from this constant obsessing about sex appeal? Was it going to be like this for the rest of my life?

Nadia leaned over and shook my arm. 'Ruby!' she whispered, with a naughty glint in her eye. 'Which boy in our class do you rate most?'

'I don't rate boys at all,' I replied icily. Nadia

rolled her eyes and pulled a silly clownish face.

'OOOO!' she hissed, looking round at Yasmin and Hannah. 'Maybe it's *girls* you like, then?' And she made it sound really sensational, like a newspaper headline.

'Shut up, you idiot!' I snapped.

'It's not girls Ruby likes,' whispered Yasmin. 'It's monkeys!'

'Are you going to marry a monkey, then?' asked Nadia with a wicked grin.

'I'm not planning to marry anybody at all,' I said, glaring at her and trying to sound superior. 'I've got better things to think about than boys, that's all – or girls, in that way.'

I tried to look out of the window and make up a story about the hills and woods we were passing through, but I could overhear everybody talking and giggling around me. Apparently there was going to be a competition – an unofficial one – to see which boy could be first to get a glimpse of Nadia's bra. It seemed to me the boy who really deserved the prize would be the one who managed *not* to see Nadia's bra. That would take real determination.

The woods got thicker. The trees almost met above our heads in a kind of magical avenue. I imagined monkeys swinging about in the canopy, looking for fruit. Nobody else on the bus seemed to be interested in the trees except me. They were all still obsessing about stupid stuff. I imagined we were in a sleigh and it was snowing and our team of dogs were pulling us at high speed down this avenue, with a pack of wolves following. We could hear the wolves panting and see their fangs glinting in the moonlight.

Suddenly an amazing castle appeared – not in my imagination. This one was real. It was huge, with battlements and a spooky tower. Even Nadia stopped talking and stared at it for a moment.

'Cool,' she said. 'I'm going to live in a castle like that when I grow up.' She plans to marry somebody hugely rich, like a rock star or something. She'll fascinate them with her horrible bras.

I'd rather live in a hut than share a castle with Nadia. I'd rather live in a lonely hut by the sea somewhere on a Scottish island. That would be great. I'd live on seaweed and seagulls' eggs, and sleep under a haunted old tartan blanket, and never see anybody. I'd be far away from girls and boys, rock stars and footballers. I'd only have mermaids for company and if the mermaids ever started talking about bras, I'd never speak to them

again and chase them off my stony beach with my trusty dog, Ross.

Before we got off the coach, Mrs Jenkins made us sit still and gave us another long pep talk about safety, and then at last we were allowed to get up. The castle lay before us, glamorous and old and haunted-looking. All the thinking I'd been doing on the bus had made me feel rather bad-tempered, but when I looked at Fairfax Castle I could only feel one thing: this was going to be amazing! Maybe we would even see a ghost!

CHAPTER 5

You've got to think of something really brilliant

ONCE WE GOT inside the castle, we were met by a young woman with glasses and very short hair. She was wearing a white shirt and chinos. She had loads of earrings. One was in the shape of a tiny toad. I liked that.

'Hey kids, today you've got to call me by my first name, which is Jade,' she said, smiling. 'Welcome to Fairfax Castle. I'm your guide for this morning. I'm going to take you on a tour of the castle. I know you've talked about this a bit already with Mrs Jenkins, so who can tell me something about what life might have been like here eight hundred years ago?'

A few people suggested things, but I was too amazed by the buildings to say anything. After a couple of minutes Jade led us to the tower right in the centre of the castle.

'OK,' said Jade. 'They started to build the castle in the 1200s – that's 800 years ago, and the first bit they built was this inner tower, called the keep.'

We gazed up at the tower. It was made of rugged stones and it looked really spooky. The waterspouts at the top were shaped like fierce animals: eagles with huge beaks and wolves with their mouths open as if they were howling. Behind the tower, grey clouds billowed and loomed like sinister smoke. It was amazing. Suddenly I heard a voice whispering in my ear.

'I've let Nadia join our gang.' It was Yasmin. 'She wants to capture Leo with us and she's totally up for it, OK?'

'Ruby! Yasmin!' Before I could even think about a reply, Mrs Jenkins' voice rang out. It was so unfair of her to say 'Ruby' when I hadn't done a thing. 'Please will you listen carefully to what Jade is saying and concentrate!' Jenko looked embarrassed as

well as cross. I moved slightly away from Yasmin.
I'd been totally concentrating on what Jade had
said. In fact, in my head I'd been halfway back to
the year 1200 already.

Now Yasmin had made me feel more mixed up
than ever. I didn't much want to be part of
Yasmin's boy-bagging gang – and now Nadia was
on board, even less so.

Jade led us up on to the castle battlements. It
was really high up. Big black birds wheeled above
us, cawing, and the wind thrashed our hair about.
We could see the countryside in all directions,
which was mostly forest, and the grassy banks

around the castle down below, and the car park with our coach in it. We could see the moat surrounding the castle and the drawbridge across the moat, which led to the main gate under the arch. We were standing on top of a huge high wall which encircled the inner yard, and in the very middle was the keep.

'So,' said Jade, 'if you were trying to capture this castle, how might you set about it?'

'You could make a catapult and throw huge rocks over the walls!' said Alice Boswell.

'After we've finished this tour,' whispered Yasmin in my ear, 'we've got to go round and fill

in our worksheets. We've got to make sure we're with Leo. I'm going to ask him how to work my digital camera. I know anyway, but I'm going to pretend it's a new one.'

For the first time in my life I wished Mrs Jenkins would tell Yasmin to shut up. But Jenko was a long way away. Because the battlements were so narrow, there was only room for about three of us to stand together, so Jenko was right at the back and she could hardly see us. Miss Roberts was looking down over the sheer drop, and Sophie's dad and Charlie's mum were talking to each other.

'You've got to think of something really brilliant, Ruby! We've got to do something amazing so Leo will want to get with us!' Yasmin went on.

'Sssssh!' I hissed. Well, somebody had to. Yasmin looked offended. I turned back to Jade. She was explaining that yes, they did have huge catapults which they used in sieges.

'Any other ideas?' she asked.

'A battering ram!' said Leo.

'That's right!' Jade beamed at him. Oh God! Everybody seemed to think Leo was as cute as hell. Except, possibly, me.

Jade went on about the enormous battering

rams they had in medieval times. I felt Yasmin move away. I tried to concentrate on what Jade was saying about armies trying to capture the castle, but I kept being distracted by Yasmin trying to capture Leo. She is a bit like a battering ram sometimes.

'However, a battering ram would be no good if the people in the castle had pulled up their drawbridge,' said Jade. 'Because then the invading army couldn't get across the moat to the door.' I privately decided to pull up my drawbridge so Yasmin couldn't get near. Never mind capturing Leo – she was also trying her best to capture *me*.

'Jade! You could swim across the moat and climb up the walls with ropes with hooks on the end!' said Toby.

'No way!' said Henry Robbins. 'The moat would be full of poo and stuff!' Some people sniggered.

'Well, you're right about the poo going into the moat,' said Jade. 'If you look along here, you can see a loo – medieval style – and of course they didn't have drains or sewers in those days, so the loo kind of jutted out above the moat, and that's where it went.'

'Plop!' said Froggo, and everybody giggled.

'Smelly!' said Hannah, shuddering.

'Yes, it was much smellier in those days,' said Jade with a rueful grin. 'Later we'll talk about what life was like then, but right now I want to concentrate on the sieges. Just for a little bit longer. It's section one of your worksheet.'

After we'd come down off the battlements, we went into the huge kitchens. The ceiling was amazingly high up. There was a very long old table all down the middle of the room, and a massive fireplace with a sort of bar across the front of it.

'This is the spit,' said Jade. Nadia giggled. To her, spit was a four-letter word. She's an idiot. 'This is how they cooked in medieval times,' Jade went on. 'You've probably seen something like it in films or on TV. They'd kill something – a deer, say, out hunting – or they'd slaughter one of their cattle, skin it and prepare it, and then fix it on this spit. It's like a huge sort of kebab. They had to keep turning the spit for hours. Who do you think did that kind of work?'

'Girls!' said Charlie. He's a bit of an idiot, too, sometimes.

'Not necessarily,' said Jade. 'In fact, in those days men worked in kitchens just as much as women. And what's more, they did a lot of the needle-work. The huge tapestries were sewn by teams of men.' Some of the boys made silly high-pitched whooping noises, but Jade ignored them.

'Who knows anything about women's lives in medieval times?' Nobody put their hand up. Jade looked a bit disappointed. 'Some people assume,' she went on, 'that girls just sat at home and weren't allowed to do anything. But women's lives could be really exciting, especially if they didn't get married.

'Women ran businesses and some of them were artists and musicians. Women were builders too – we've got paintings showing them helping to build the great cathedrals. And one woman in particular was a warrior. She led an army. Does anybody know who I'm talking about?'

Nobody did.

'I'll give you a clue,' said Jade. 'She was French.'

'Amelie Mauresmo,' said Leo. Some people laughed. I'm a bit of a tennis fan and I love Amelie Mauresmo, but I was kind of irritated that Leo mentioned her. Yasmin giggled loudly. She was hoping Leo would be impressed that she liked his joke (even though I was sure she had never even heard of Amelie Mauresmo), that they evidently had the same sense of humour, that – maybe – they were made for each other and marriage could only follow.

'No,' said Jade with a kind of not-completely-real smile, 'not Amelie. Joan of Arc. She dressed as a man and led the French army against the English – and she was captured by the English and burnt at the stake.'

I felt sad about Joan, even if she had been French and fighting against us. History is full of such sad, cruel stuff. Then, all of a sudden, my tummy rumbled – really loudly – and everybody laughed. I felt embarrassed.

'You're right,' said Jade, smiling at me. 'My talk's gone on long enough. I think it's about lunchtime.

But just before I leave you, I must warn you about one or two things – OK, Mrs Jenkins?' Then Jade went into one of those little safety pep talks again, about how the castle was full of dangers. I was getting really bored with grown-ups being so jittery about everything. Do they think we're idiots or something?

Although I was hungry, I wasn't looking forward to the rest of the lunchbreak. I'd have to watch Yasmin pretending she didn't understand how a digital camera worked, just so she could get with Leo. It was almost enough to put me off my cheese and tomato sarnies.

CHAPTER 6
I'm gonna eat you!

FOR OUR PICNIC lunch, we went and sat on one of the grassy banks outside the castle. We had our worksheets and Mrs Jenkins said that after we'd finished our lunch we'd have half an hour to fill them in before we went to visit the forest.

'Let's sit under that tree!' yelled Yasmin. It was quite hot by now. 'I've got some factor twenty-five sun cream if anybody wants some!' She looked at Leo, hoping he'd lie down beside her and whip his shirt off so she could rub her cream all over his back. But Leo was joking with Charlie and Toby and he hadn't even heard her.

'Listen,' hissed Yasmin, once we'd all started in on our picnics, 'we've got to come up with some really amazing things to do so Leo will think we're cool. Everybody who's a member of our gang has got to think of a brilliant idea.'

I didn't want to think of something amazing to do. I just wanted to eat my cheese and tomato sandwich (my favourite, although egg and tomato comes a close second).

'What do you mean, amazing?' asked Hannah.

'Just something, well, kind of daring, maybe,' said Yasmin. My heart sank. I'm such a wuss. I don't like taking risks.

'What – now? Today?' asked Nadia, chewing with her mouth open (I so hate that). 'Or back at school?'

'Either, either,' said Yasmin, waggling her hands about. 'It doesn't matter. Just as long as Leo thinks we're cool.'

Leo was sitting out in the sun with a group of boys.

'Let's move and sit next to them,' said Nadia, getting up on her knees.

'No! Wait!' said Yas, pulling her down again.

'We've got to discuss our brilliant ideas first. Ruby! What shall we do?'

I shrugged. Yasmin looked irritated. Then she turned to Lauren.

'Maybe we could . . . pretend we're horses?' suggested Lauren. She didn't look too confident about her idea. I like Lauren, but her suggestion was rubbish.

'If we start galloping about and neighing, we'll only look insane,' snapped Yasmin.

'I'll get them to star in a movie,' said Hannah. She'd brought her mum's video camera.

'Brilliant idea!' said Yasmin. 'What movie would it be?'

'*Braveheart?*' suggested Lauren. She likes films with a lot of horses and riding in them. 'Or *Lord of the Rings*. Or *Harry Potter*.'

'Or just a totally new movie!' said Hannah, finishing her lunch and reaching for her video cam.

I just went on eating my sandwiches and watching and listening. I felt as if I didn't belong. The idea of making a film was fantastic, but making a film just to get some random boys to think we're cool – that was garbage.

Hannah switched on her video camera and pointed it at Yasmin. Yas struck a glamorous pose

and pursed her lips up in a pout. Hannah turned towards me. I stuck my tongue out. The camera moved on to Lauren. Lauren covered her face with her hands and giggled helplessly, shouting, 'Take it away!'

Finally Hannah zoomed in on Nadia – and guess what! Nadia whipped up her T-shirt and flashed her bra at the camera! Right there in broad daylight, on a school trip, with loads of people all around us! Luckily it happened so quickly, nobody seemed to notice except us.

'Right,' said Hannah. 'Now I've got the bra shot in the can, I'm going to shoot everybody else.' She crept slowly across the grass, holding the camera to her eye. As people realised she was filming, they pulled faces and posed in different ways. She even went up to where Mrs Jenkins was sitting and filmed her. Mrs Jenkins did a grim little smile at the camera, and then said, 'That's enough, Hannah!' and waved her off again.

Hannah moved on towards the group of boys – Froggo, Max, Charlie, Toby and the dreamboat himself, Leo. Yasmin got up and scrambled after her. Lauren and I stayed sitting under the tree.

'OK, guys!' yelled Yasmin. 'Time for your Hollywood screen test!'

Froggo jumped up right away and started doing macho poses, pretending to flex his muscles.

'I'm Mr Universe!' he said. Max got up beside him and they went into a pretend fight (what else?). It was kind of slow motion and arty, a bit like something from a kung-foo movie.

'Mr Universe versus Sir Lancelot!' shouted Toby.

Froggo pretended to stab Max with an invisible dagger, and Max died in slow motion, rolling around on the grass and choking for ages.

Then Hannah and Yasmin sat down with the boys.

'Cool camera,' said Charlie. Hannah held it out towards Charlie and Leo. She was hoping Leo would take it, but he didn't move, and Charlie grabbed it instead.

'How does it work?' said Charlie. Hannah showed him. Leo watched. It was quite ironical, really – the opposite of what Yasmin had planned.

Once he'd got the hang of the camera, Charlie had a go with it.

'Film us!' yelled Yasmin, putting her arm around Hannah and trying to look festive and partyish.

Charlie didn't seem to hear her – he didn't take any notice, anyway. He just kept pointing the thing at other boys, zooming right in doing close-ups while they pulled horrible faces.

'Would you like a tomato-flavoured crisp, Ruby?' asked Lauren. 'I'm not very hungry.' We shared a packet, watching while Yasmin and Hannah tried to persuade Charlie to make a movie out of them. 'Yasmin is fantastic, isn't she?' said Lauren with a sigh, as if she herself could never be so fantastic.

'She's OK,' I muttered. 'Sometimes she's just stupid, though.'

Yasmin got up and stared at the horizon, pulling a sad face like an actress in one of those old silent movies. Hannah jumped up to join her.

'We're waiting for our husbands to come back from the crusades!' said Yasmin.

'And,' yelled Hannah, 'we're being held captive by a fearsome dragon! We need a knight to come and fight the dragon!'

'I'm the dragon!' shouted Froggo, and he made a horrible burping slurping noise. Lauren started laughing. Even I smiled.

'Froggo is so funny, isn't he?' said Lauren.

Froggo pulled a fearsome dragon face and started prowling about, spitting and roaring at people.

'Help! Help!' called Yasmin, wringing her hands. She was totally in character. She's good at drama, I

have to admit it. 'Are there no brave knights who will come and slay this dragon? Sir Toby! Sir Max! Sir Leo!'

'I don't think Leo is going to rescue her,' whispered Lauren. 'He looks embarrassed.'

Nobody was going to rescue her. Froggo the dragon advanced on her, roaring. Hannah ran off, screaming and giggling.

'Hard luck, Princess!' growled Froggo. 'The knights are all busy! So I'm gonna eat you! Pass the ketchup!'

Froggo pretended to take a huge bite out of Yasmin's neck. Charlie was filming the whole thing. Yasmin tried to fight the dragon off for a while, but then she decided the best thing to do was to die as glamorously as possible. So she slumped down gracefully on to the grass, pulling a tragic and beautiful face of torment.

Unfortunately for Yasmin, I could see quite clearly that Leo had got bored and was starting to read through his worksheet. So she'd died glamorously in vain.

CHAPTER 7

Oh, shut up about all that stuff, Ruby!

NOW IT WAS time to complete our worksheets, and we were divided up into groups. Our group was Yasmin, Hannah, Lauren, Nadia and me. We were allowed to go anywhere in the castle as long as we didn't run or make a loud noise. There were loads of really spooky, wonderful places Jade had shown us on our tour, and there was also a kind of museum in one of the chambers, where there was an exhibition with pictures and models all about how the castle was built, and how it held out against invading armies.

The boys went off towards the museum, because most of the questions on the worksheet were about the sieges, when the castle was being attacked. Also boys like that sort of thing. Attacking, being attacked. I hate all that. OK, I would defend myself if I had to. I've kicked my bro Joe a few times. But I only did it because he was pulling my hair so hard, it felt as if my whole head was screaming.

'Let's go up on the battlements again!' I said. It was so cool up there. I wanted to stare out from high up, with the wind in my hair. Yasmin and Nadia were making up some silly rhymes about going to the loo in the thirteenth century, and Hannah was telling Lauren about a castle she'd visited with her parents in Wales, so I was sort of on my own. But that was fine by me. In my head I was back in the thirteenth century already.

We walked across the inner courtyard to where the staircase was. It was in a turret – one of those spiral stone staircases that seems to go on for ever. The steps were kind of worn down because people had been going up there for hundreds of years. The others were still all rabbiting away about stupid things, so I ignored them and went on ahead.

About every fifteen steps or so there was a slit in the wall for people to shoot arrows out of. I peeped out of one. I saw a family on the grassy slope across the moat, packing up their picnic. The mother was shaking the picnic cloth, the dad was packing things into the basket. The kids were fighting with pretend plastic swords. There must have been kids living here 800 years ago. I wondered what they had been like.

I went on climbing. As I got higher I could hear the wind moaning around the stones. I imagined I was a medieval secret agent. No, I was Joan of Arc. No, being Joan would involve killing. I was a man called Merlin who could make powerful spells. I was wearing a long blue velvet cloak and outside it was snowing. I had to get some snow for a spell I was working on. The spell was going to be a kind of magic drink and anyone who had even a tiny little sip would stay ten years old for ever. Or if they were older, they would go back to being ten years old.

At last I reached the top, and climbed out through a very low little stone arch on to the battlements. There were a few people strolling about. Miss Roberts was up there, keeping an eye on us.

'Hello, Ruby,' she said. 'Be careful up here. Hold

the handrail and don't run.' I nodded. I didn't mind her nagging at me. This time we were free to go wherever we liked. We didn't have to stand still like last time, listening politely to Jade's talk, all crammed up together with everybody, and Yasmin whispering in my ear about boys, boys, boys.

I walked along with the wind whistling in my hair and tugging at my jacket, and the others followed me. We came to a corner where there was a big stone step where you could peep out from between the battlements and imagine what it would have been like making spells in the snow, in the year 1399. I took a few photographs for the competition.

'Ruby,' whispered Yasmin. 'I've got a brilliant idea about how to get with Leo. You'll never guess!' I didn't bother to answer because I wasn't a bit interested, but I couldn't really say so because then Yasmin would explode and it would ruin the day. I kind of shrugged, which was the only way I could pretend I was still a tiny bit interested.

'I'm going to tell him I can read people's fortunes from looking at their palms!' said Yasmin excitedly. 'Then he'll sit down with me, and I'll get to hold his hand!'

'She's going to do it on the bus on the way

home!' said Hannah. 'She's been practising on me, and she's said I'm going to be a film star!'

Nobody can tell anybody's future by just looking at the palm of their hand, I thought. I didn't say anything, though, because I didn't want them to think I was grouchy.

'Yasmin, read Ruby's palm!' Hannah went on.

'Yes, come on, Ruby!' nagged Yasmin. 'Stop staring at those blinking trees!'

I turned round and held out my hand. Yasmin grabbed it and stared at it.

'You're going to marry a tall dark man and have three kids!' she said.

'I *so* am not!' I retorted.

'Yes, you are!' Yasmin insisted, laughing. 'Two girls and a very, very big-headed boy.'

'No,' I said firmly. 'I'm not!' I felt quite cross for some reason. It was stupid of me, because I knew Yasmin was only kidding.

Suddenly another group came towards us: it was Sophie's dad with four of the boys in our class, including Tom Whistler, who is majorly stupid and sometimes calls me 'monkeyface'. Oh no! I so wished I could have this place to myself. It was bad enough having Yasmin and co gassing away about boys all the time. I wanted to wallow in wizards and spells and history and snow and cloaks, but I knew if we stayed where we were, Tom Whistler would spoil it with one of his so-called funny remarks.

'Let's go,' I said irritably, pulling my hand away. We could get down without having to push past the group with Sophie's dad, because the battlements went all round the castle and there were other stone staircases we could use. As we descended again I tried to get back into my medieval daydream, but it was no use. Yasmin and Hannah were jabbering all the time.

'I'm going to have six kids,' said Yasmin. 'Three boys and three girls.'

'I'm going to have just girls,' said Hannah. 'I might have four, or I might have five, and they're going to be called Kylie and Morgan and Venus and Fern and Paris.'

I think Paris is a stupid name for a girl. You might as well call somebody Birmingham.

'What about Sienna and Angelina?' said Yasmin. 'You told me they were your favourite names!'

'Oh, yeah!' said Hannah, laughing. 'I'll have to have seven, then!'

'What are you going to call your kids, Ruby?' asked Yasmin, as we arrived at the bottom of the stone staircase.

I couldn't believe Yas and Hannah could be yakking away about something so stupid while they were climbing down that weird spooky spiral staircase, with the echoes and the howling wind and everything. They were talking as if they were just anywhere. Were they deaf and blind? Was I the only one who noticed things?

'Yeah,' said Hannah, 'what are you going to call your children, Ruby?'

'I told you, I'm not going to have any children!' I snapped. 'Remember what Mrs Jenkins said about overpopulation? If you have seven kids, and each of your kids has seven kids, that'd be forty-nine people taking up the space where just one person had been before!'

'Oh, shut up about all that stuff, Ruby!' groaned Yasmin. 'Nagging and preaching all the time! It's so, like, *boring*!'

I ignored her. If Yasmin thought the environment was boring, it just showed what an airhead she was. I was beginning to think I was the only person who really understood about the important things in life. It was a bit tragic really.

CHAPTER 8
Spooky!

WE ALL ASSEMBLED at the foot of the keep, and Mrs Jenkins counted us and gave us another little pep talk, and then told us it was time for our visit to the forest and as usual we were to walk not run. As we made our way out of the castle and along a path into the forest, everybody was gassing away about the photo competition.

'Hannah's going to win,' Yasmin was saying. 'She's got an amazing view looking up at the tower!'

'No, Yas,' insisted Hannah, 'you're going to win with that shot of the suit of armour! Spooky!'

'Froggo's got a close-up of Nadia's bra!' said Max. 'He's going to post it on the internet too!'

Nadia looked kind of proud when he said this, although if I was her I'd be feeling sick with embarrassment. I looked up at the trees. Nobody else was paying them any attention. They met above the path to form a kind of magic tunnel. It felt like another world.

After walking along the woodland path for a little way, we came to a big hut called Information Centre. Inside there was a central area with display screens and books and diagrams. At the end was a door and Mrs Jenkins led us through into a sort of classroom. My heart sank. Not another lecture!

Jade had been OK, but I don't like guided tours. I like going around on my own and finding things out if I want to know them. This afternoon would have been amazing if we'd just been allowed to walk through the forest completely free. Instead we had to sit through another talk. It was no different from being at school really.

'Sit down, everybody, and get out your second worksheet,' said Mrs Jenkins. 'Will will be with us in a minute.'

'Will will!' whispered Froggo. 'Will he?'

'Will will bring his willy!' whispered Max.

I looked away and pretended I hadn't heard them. Usually I love Froggo's jokes, but he seemed a bit stupid today. Everybody did.

A man came in and walked down to the front of the class. He was about the same height as Dad but younger and more muscly. His hair was brown and very curly and his eyes were kind of green. He was wearing a green T-shirt, combat trousers and big strong boots.

'Hi guys,' he said. 'My name's Will O'Hara and I'm a forester here at Fairfax. Trees are the most

amazing living things. Without trees, there could be no life on earth. Does anybody know why?'

Everybody knew this, because Jenko had explained a couple of weeks ago about how trees make oxygen and absorb carbon dioxide, so they create an atmosphere which we animals can breathe, and get rid of the carbon we breathe out, thus helping to combat global warming. I always knew trees were brilliant, but once she'd told us about this I felt kind of proud of them, as if a member of my family had turned out to be a genius.

'OK,' Will went on, 'I'm just going to fill you in with a few facts about trees and then you'll be free to walk about and see stuff for yourselves. So just bear with me for a couple of minutes and let's think about trees. Take a look around you and put your hand up if you can see anything that's made of a tree.'

'This building,' said Max.

'The furniture,' said Froggo.

'Pencils,' said Hannah.

'Paper,' said Charlie.

It seemed almost everything around us was made of wood. Will showed us a few more things: the handle of his penknife, a salad bowl and salad servers, and a basket.

'Baskets are woven from willow,' he said. 'That's another sort of tree. Corks in wine bottles – cork is a tree that grows in Portugal. Actually we could spend hours talking about all the things that are made out of trees, but I know you want to go out and get on with your exploring bit, so let's move on. OK, I work as a forester, what do you think that involves?'

None of us really knew, so Will explained that a forest had to be looked after, or it would just be a horrible wilderness of trees all growing close together in a tangly mess.

'It would be the kind of place where nothing could live,' he said. 'And it would be mostly fast-growing trees, kind of like weeds, and they'd choke out the more slow-growing majestic ones.'

I loved the word *majestic*. I was going to make sure I used it in my worksheet. Will had a nice husky voice and as he talked he waved his hands about a lot and smiled nervously.

He told us about how the foresters have to plant the kind of trees they want, thin them out after several years, watch out for fungus and other kinds of tree illness, and when the trees get old, make sure they're felled safely.

'OK, we all know that in some other countries

the rainforest is being destroyed, but who knows what sustainably managed plantations are?' He wrote the words on the board. I liked his writing. It was italic.

'Sustainable means it can go on for ever and ever,' said Max.

'Amen,' added Froggo. A few people giggled.

'Yeah, amen, I agree,' said Will. 'If a forest is properly managed by foresters, the trees will be felled when they reach maturity, and more young ones planted. So the plantation can go on and on and it's always being renewed.'

'Why do you have to fell them?' asked Yasmin. 'It's sad.'

'On a plantation like that, the trees are just a crop,' said Will. 'People have to be able to make money out of them, so they can buy food and clothes and educate their children.'

Then he told us that at Fairfax they had a special section of the woodland called an arboretum, which was a collection of lots of different rare trees from all over the world, and of course they were never felled until they got old or sick.

'And don't forget, guys,' he said as his talk ended, 'treat trees with respect. They can be dangerous. Kids are killed by trees sometimes. Never go under a tree in a storm. And as you walk around our woods today, keep to the paths and don't abuse the trees – don't break bits off, don't carve your names on their trunks and, of course, don't even think about climbing them.

'We foresters have to climb trees sometimes to cut off a rotten branch or something, and when we do we have to wear a whole lot of protective gear, safety helmets and stuff, and ropes and harnesses. OK – I'm done now, so just remember what I said: enjoy the rest of your visit to Fairfax Forest, and never take trees for granted.'

Yasmin put up her hand. Will looked a bit surprised, because he'd been about to go, but he paused.

'OK, just one question,' he said.

'Ruby doesn't take trees for granted,' said Yasmin. 'She loves trees and she's even got a tree house in her bedroom, haven't you, Ruby?'

She turned to me. Everybody was looking at me. Will looked straight at me for a moment and his eyes were greener than ever. I felt myself go bright red. I couldn't speak. I just nodded.

'A tree house in your bedroom?' asked Will, looking puzzled and grinning at me. 'How does that work exactly? I can't get my head round it.'

I explained how my bro Joe and my dad had built a kind of bed-platform for me, including some real branches from one of Yasmin's trees which had had to be cut down, and how I climbed up a rope ladder every night to go to bed.

'How amazing!' said Will. 'I've got a little girl called Rosie, and when she's older I might organise something for her like that – if you don't mind me stealing your idea?'

'It wasn't my idea,' I said. 'They did it as a surprise for me for my last birthday. It was my brother's idea, and a girl at Ashcroft School called Holly. She designs things.'

'Well, that's amazing,' said Will. 'It's a brilliant idea. Oh, I forgot to say, we've got a club here called the Young Rangers if anyone wants to join. We organise environmental things here all year round – nature walks, bird watching, loads of exciting stuff. Anyway, you've been a great group to talk to. You'll have to excuse me now. I've got an appointment with some V.I.T.s – Very Important Trees.' And with a big grin he was gone, before we could clap or anything. I wondered if I would ever see him again. I hoped so, because he was sort of inspiring.

CHAPTER 9
You're so moody!

I WAS ANNOYED with Yasmin though. 'You idiot, Yasmin!' I whispered as we packed up our stuff. 'What did you want to mention my name for? I felt, like, totally embarrassed!'

'I was only saying how great you are, Ruby, you muppet!' snapped Yasmin. 'Letting him know you were crazy about trees! You weren't going to say anything, were you? Cos you're, like, being moody and stuff!'

'I am not being moody!' I growled moodily. 'And

when I want my tree house to be mentioned, I'll do it myself, thanks very much!'

'Well, you can go and eat your own bottom!' Yasmin glared at me. Her eyes flashed and she looked dangerous. I knew she was longing for a row with yelling and everything, but she could hardly have one here on the school trip. So she just flounced out. Hannah and Lauren and Nadia had already gone out together. I was on my own.

I pulled on my jacket and looked back at the whiteboard. Will's writing was still there: *sustainably managed plantations*. I liked that italic style. Holly's writing is a bit like that, probably because she's gothic. Then I sighed, picked up my clipboard and bag and trudged out.

Everybody had assembled just outside the Information Centre and Mrs Jenkins was counting us. She'd already done this several times. She was obviously scared that somebody would get lost or be hurt. I wonder if teachers enjoy school trips or hate them. I'll have to ask my dad. Because he's a geography teacher he often has to go away on field trips and stay in youth hostels, so he has to count people night and day for nearly a week.

'Now,' said Mrs Jenkins. 'Stay in the same

groups you were in before. I want everyone back here at 3.30. You've got till then to walk around the forest paths, visit the arboretum and fill in your worksheets. Stay in your groups. I don't want anybody going off on their own. If you stay on the paths it's impossible to get lost. Every path has got little signposts on it and there are red arrows pointing back in the direction of the Information Centre. Now, has every group got at least one watch?'

We all had watches, of course. 'I want you back here at the Information Centre at half past three,' Jenko went on. 'All right. Any questions?'

She looked around. There were no questions. Everybody wanted to explore.

'See you back here at 3.30, then,' said Mrs Jenkins. 'And don't forget your photos for the competition.'

'Where shall we go?' asked Nadia. 'Look! The boys are going off down by those pine trees. Let's follow them!'

'Yay!' said Yasmin. 'I'm going to be Maid Marian and Leo's going to be Robin Hood!'

Yasmin was obviously going to spend the whole time following boys and Nadia was going to be obsessing about her bra. I felt so low I could hard-

ly speak – but I wasn't going to talk to her anyway,
so it didn't matter.

'Did you see Joss's dress at that concert last
weekend?' said Nadia. 'It was, like, totally hideous.
Like curtains or something. I like her hair though,
she's amazingly beautiful, and she's got these legs
to totally die for, but her taste in clothes is so hip-
pyish it isn't true! Who do you rate most: Beyoncé
or Angelina?'

'Beyoncé,' said Yasmin.

'Angelina,' said Hannah. 'What about you,
Lauren?'

'I like Lily Allen,' said Lauren.

I shrugged, looking up at the trees with a serious expression on my face as if I was thinking about global warming.

'Ruby! Stop sulking!' said Yasmin. 'Who do you like best?'

'I don't like anyone best,' I snapped.

Yasmin flashed her eyes and started to look stressy.

'Listen, listen!' said Nadia, 'Do you think that what's-her-name on *EastEnders* has had a boob job? She's way more busty than she used to be.' Nadia glanced down at her own chest for a moment, as if to check if she, too, might be way more busty now than she had been this morning.

'God, Angelina is such a legend, though, adopting all those kids and everything!' sighed Hannah. 'Imagine having her as your mum!'

I looked sternly ahead and frowned to show these trashy airheads I was a whole different species from them. I wasn't going to think about celebs and their boob jobs. I was thinking about saving the earth.

'We've got to identify seven different species of trees and mark them in on the map,' I said in an important husky voice a bit like Will's.

'Oh, you do that, Ruby. I'm no good at that sort

of thing,' said Nadia, whipping out a little mirror and checking her eyebrows. 'If you work out the stuff for the worksheet, I'll let you have a go with my lip gloss.'

'I don't want your stupid lip gloss,' I snapped.

'It's got an SPF of twenty-five!' said Yasmin, who was already trying some. 'If you want to get burnt lips, that's up to you.' And she put some on. OK, it might have had an SPF of twenty-five, but it was basically sparkly pink lipstick.

'You look stupid wearing lipstick in a wood!' I sneered.

'It is anti-sunburn, Ruby, really,' said Lauren, trying to calm everybody down. But Yasmin lost it.

'You're so moody!' she snarled. 'Stop being so horrible, Ruby! You're ruining it for everybody!'

'Well, you're all ruining it for me!' I snapped. I'd had enough. I hated them all. I ran off down a little side path that was almost hidden by some bushes.

'Ruby!' I heard Yasmin yell. 'Don't be silly! Come back!'

I ignored her and ran on. I left the path and hid in some bushes. I could still hear their voices.

'Oh, leave her,' said Nadia. 'She'll soon come back when she's finished sulking.'

I heard them walk away. Their voices got quieter and quieter. I was glad they had gone. The silence was divine. I was totally alone. I came out of the bushes and looked around. It was much darker down this path. The trees were huge and they cast deep shade. At last I relaxed and began to feel happy.

I got out my worksheet and soon I'd filled out the names of seven different trees: oak, ash, beech, horse chestnut, maple, birch, hazel. Then I added three more just to show off: larch, juniper, willow. I marked them in on my map and wrote their names out in italic-looking writing, like Will's. I love the names of trees. If I ever do have a daughter, I might call her Hazel or Rowan.

Once I'd finished the worksheet, I was free to explore. I was totally alone. I couldn't even hear people's voices any more. Not even Froggo's. They'd moved off to another part of the forest. I was alone – but I didn't feel lonely. The trees all around me moved in the breeze, sighing quietly.

I walked until I came to the hugest tree I had ever seen. Just looking up into its branches made me dizzy. I lay down under it and looked up at the sky. You could see little patches of blue sky and white cloud and sunbeams. The leaves all seemed to be dancing.

Then I heard voices: men's voices. I felt a tiny stab of fear. Mrs Jenkins had said she didn't want anybody going off on their own. And what did Mum always say? 'Never go off to lonely places all by yourself.'

I scrambled to my feet. I didn't want anybody to see me and the men's voices were getting nearer. They could be kidnappers – anything.

I nipped round the back of the huge tree and hid. And then I noticed something. There was a branch round the back that was really low and inviting. You could, in theory, climb up this *majestic* tree, starting right here.

I didn't stop to think. I didn't have time. I just threw my bag into a nearby bush and swung myself up on to the lowest branch.

WOOF! WOOF!

CHAPTER 10
Shut up, you idiot!

I T WAS A REALLY easy tree to climb.
The branches could have been designed for it.
Even though my camera was still slung round my
shoulders, in a few seconds I was quite high up –
way above the heads of anybody walking below. I
saw a dog come round the corner of the path. It
paused by the bush where I'd thrown my bag, and
sniffed. Then it looked up into my tree and
barked. I cringed back against the trunk. The two
men then appeared.

They were talking away and didn't seem even

to notice the dog barking. They didn't look much like kidnappers, not from above anyway, but you never can tell. I held on tight to the trunk until they had gone right out of sight, taking their pesky dog with them.

It was quiet after that, except for the wind whispering in the leaves all around me. I just stayed where I was for a bit. The tree creaked gently like an old sailing ship on the ocean. Birds flitted about around my head and beneath my feet. I knew I was breaking the rules by being up there, but it felt so right. For the first time that day I felt really chilled out and happy.

I was totally at home. And it didn't feel dangerous really. This was such an easy tree to climb. It was so huge and strong, it had obviously been there for more than a hundred years, and would probably still be there a hundred years from now. No way was a branch going to break. It was like being held by a great, big, strong, friendly giant.

I knew I must be very cautious, but I decided to go up a bit higher. Now I was climbing slowly and very, very carefully, but I couldn't stop. I had to get to the top. Gradually there were fewer branches and the clusters of leaves were not so thick. I was able to look down on smaller trees.

Suddenly I was there, right at the very top. Clinging to a strong branch, I gazed down on an amazing sight. The view took my breath away. All around was the canopy of treetops, and right ahead of me the distant towers of the castle rose into the sky. Sunlight was slanting down through some huge glowing clouds. It made the walls of the castle and the tops of the trees look golden, and they seemed to float above the earth, like a glimpse of a vanished world.

Very carefully, holding tight to the branch with my right arm, I got my camera out of its case and switched it on. The funny little buzz it makes sounded strange up there, where there was only the wind, the creaking of branches and the twittering of birds.

I took a photo of the castle looming proudly over the tree canopy. Then I put the camera carefully away and just hung there for a while. It was a total thrill to be so high in a tree. I'd climbed trees before but never a majestic one like that. I felt as if I'd left all Nadia and Yasmin's stressy stuff behind me, on the ground.

I completely lost track of time, swaying gently in the arms of the tree. Monkeys must feel like that, safe in their airy home. I wished Will was with me to show me things about the tree that I didn't know yet. I did feel a bit bad about climbing one of his trees against the rules, and without the proper equipment, but still, it was amaaaazing, so I couldn't regret doing it. It was the best time I'd *ever* had.

I was just beginning to think about coming down when I heard voices. This time I recognised them. Nadia's pesky yowling. Yasmin's shrill giggle. Hannah's non-stop chatter. They were somewhere nearby, and coming closer.

They weren't going to spoil my amazing moment. I was so high up now that the people below me looked very small. Suddenly Yasmin appeared, skipping along the path down there. I could only see the top of her head really. Nadia was taking photos of Hannah, who kept posing by various bushes and trees. Lauren was carrying the worksheet.

'This is a lovely little tree, look!' she called, going up to a flowery tree right next to where I'd left my bag in the bush. I held my breath. I prayed.

'Oh my God!' shouted Hannah in a panicky voice. My prayers have been answered once or twice in my life, but this time God was obviously busy somewhere else. 'Look! There's a bag in that bush! – Oh no! It's Ruby's!'

Hannah reached into the bush and dragged my bag out. They all stood around looking at it for a moment. They were still and quiet. The bag lay on the ground like something dead. Then Nadia started screaming and flapping her arms about.

'Ohmigod! Ohmigod! She's been kidnapped!' she yelled.

'Don't be stupid, Nadia!' said Yasmin. 'She's probably just left it there for safe keeping while she went to get some photos or something. She won't be far away. Ruby! . . . Ruby!' Yasmin was looking all around, and calling at the top of her voice.

I clung on tight to the tree branch. I was furious with them for finding my bag and panicking. I wasn't going to reply. They'd ruined my magic moment. I didn't want *anybody* to know I'd climbed this tree. Not just because it was against the rules. Because it had been such an amazing thing to do.

'Ruby! . . . Ruby! . . . Ruby!' They kept calling. They peered in all directions, but they didn't think of looking above their heads. They wouldn't have seen me even if they had looked up, because I was far, far above them and my body was pressed close to the branch.

'Oh my God!' said Nadia. 'What if she really has been kidnapped?'

'Shut up, you idiot!' snapped Yasmin. 'We've got to go and tell Mrs Jenkins.'

'Should we leave the bag here?' asked Hannah. Their voices floated up to me, clear as anything. I knew now what it was like to be a wild creature hiding from human invaders. 'What if Ruby comes back and can't find it? She'll panic and she might go looking for it and miss the bus!'

'We'll leave a note,' said Yasmin. She scribbled something on a piece of paper and stuck it on the branch where my bag had been. Then she picked up my bag and they all ran off.

Suddenly the forest wasn't a wonderful, lonely paradise: it was full of trouble. Now I was in a fix. I climbed down the tree, my heart pounding. I had to think of something convincing to tell Jenko, double quick.

I dropped down off the last branch on to the ground and paused for a moment to look up into the majestic living thing I'd been so close to. I patted its trunk. *Thanks*, I whispered. *I'll be back*.

I tore Yasmin's note off the bush and screwed it up without even reading it. I put it in my pocket and walked quickly back the way I'd come. There was no point in running. Yasmin and co had gone off ages ago, before I'd even started my climb down. They'd probably be showing the bag to Jenko right now. I had to work out what to say.

I was in big, big, big, big trouble.

CHAPTER 11

What is the meaning of this?

WHEN I ARRIVED at the Information Centre, everybody was milling about, showing one another their photos and comparing their worksheets. Yasmin, Hannah, Lauren and Nadia were talking to Mrs Jenkins and the moment Jenko saw me was terrible. We locked eyes – hers were burning with irritation.

'Ruby!' said Mrs Jenkins in a commanding voice. 'Come here! What is the meaning of this?'

Everybody turned round and looked at me. Why did she have to make it into such a drama? I felt myself go bright red.

Jenko was holding my bag up in a disgusted kind of way, as if it was a sack of poo or something. There was no need for her to be so sarcastic. I hated her. I walked right up to her and looked her in the eye. She is frightening, but I was getting sick and tired of being frightened.

'Somebody stole my bag,' I said, trying to sound fierce and annoyed. Mrs Jenkins' eyes flashed.

'Hannah found your bag just thrown in a bush, apparently,' said Jenko. 'And you were nowhere to be seen. Where were you? Why did you leave your group?'

I felt a surge of rage. I was going to embarrass her, and embarrass them all, instead of being ashamed of myself all the time.

'I was taking a toilet break,' I said boldly.

Jenko looked a bit surprised. For a split second I saw her kind of flinch.

'Without your bag?' She raised an eyebrow and tried to make me feel small.

'I wasn't far away,' I said. 'The first bush I went in was too near the path. I just left my bag in there and went to another bush.'

'Why didn't you answer when we called, Ruby?' asked Yasmin.

'Would you?' I said, looking challenging at her. 'If you were having a pee under a bush?' Then I turned back to Mrs Jenkins and let the tail-end of what I'd said kind of drift over her a bit, so that everybody in the class could imagine her having a pee under a bush.

Jenko pulled an irritated face. I felt hard and hot inside. People were sniggering, but I didn't care. I don't think they were sniggering at me.

'There are toilets right here at the Information Centre,' she snapped. 'Next time please behave like a civilised human being, not a wild animal.' She handed me my bag.

We lined up to get on the bus. I was still kind of boiling inside, but I felt pleased, too, as if I'd won. Jenko had called me a wild animal, but as far as I was concerned that was a compliment.

'Ruby!' Yasmin pulled at my sleeve. I turned to her. To my amazement, her eyes were full of tears. 'Oh, Ruby!' she said. 'I'm so glad you're safe! It was so horrid and frightening when we saw your bag! I didn't know what had happened to you . . . I was afraid I might never see you again!' And she threw her arms around me and gave me a hug.

I was astonished. Yasmin had been so worried about me, she was crying with relief that I was safe! Amazing thought! I hugged her back – briefly – and felt all the rage ebb away.

'Fancy peeing under a bush and then telling Jenko all about it like that!' Yasmin whispered, squeezing my hand and smiling through her slightly teary eyes. 'Ruby, you are a legend!' If Yasmin knew what I'd really been doing, I'd be more legendary still.

'You're the one who's the legend!' I said. 'Keeping your cool and organising everything! Even leaving me that note on the bush! Are you going to be a policewoman when you grow up, or something?'

'I could never be a policewoman!' giggled Yasmin. 'I don't rate the uniform!' She gave me another little hug. It felt cosy being best friends again. 'Sit with me on the way home,' said Yas. 'I won't talk about Leo any more. I know you're fed up with it and so am I and I don't think he's interested in girls anyway. He wouldn't let me read his palm. I think he's gay.'

'Don't be silly, Yas,' I said. 'You know what boys are like. He's probably just obsessing with level eighty-eight on his Game Boy or something.'

Yasmin looked a bit relieved, and gave Leo a quick glance. I could tell she hadn't completely got over her little crush, but she was working on it.

'So,' I said, once we were back on the bus, 'how did you get on with your photos?'

'I took loads of boring old castle walls and things,' whispered Yasmin, 'but my favourite one is of Lauren being frightened on the battlements!' She giggled. Lauren was feeling better now, so it wasn't a big deal. 'Look at this!' giggled Yasmin, scrolling through her photos. 'She looks *green*!'

'I can't stand heights,' said Lauren.

'Let's hope your future boyfriends aren't too tall, then!' grinned Nadia.

Next day at school we all gave our photos in. I chose the one I'd taken from the top of the tree. It had a kind of glow that I loved. Somehow the light was just right. The photo competition was going to be judged by Mrs Wakefield, the head teacher. She's big and fat and pale and frightening, like a gigantic fish on legs. She took our photos home with her on a CD and went through them all.

Next day Mrs Wakefield came in and showed loads of our photos on the big video screen. She said something nice and appreciative about everybody's photos. I waited and waited for mine to appear. We all knew she would leave the best three till last.

'Here's the third-prize photo,' she said in her deep, sad voice (she always sounds sad, even at happy times). 'Toby's photo of the window in the dungeon. It's quite hard taking photos indoors, and Toby's managed to capture the gloomy atmosphere in the castle really well. Look at the sunbeams slanting across. Well done, Toby!'

We clapped. Mrs Wakefield moved on to the second-best photo. It was Hannah's view looking up at the keep.

'This is a terrific photo,' said Mrs Wakefield. 'Well done, Hannah. The tower looms over us, you see, as if it's about the fall on us, and the dark clouds in the background make it very atmospheric.' We all clapped Hannah.

'And now,' said Mrs Wakefield in her dramatic voice, 'for the winner.'

My photo appeared! The view from the top of the tree with the forest canopy and the castle all glowing with golden light! It looked a hundred times better blown up on our big screen. Everybody gasped. My heart gave a huge leap of excitement.

'This is Ruby's photo,' said Mrs Wakefield, 'and it makes me wish I had been on that trip with you. It's a magnificent view, isn't it? Well done, Ruby!' She smiled at me. Everybody looked at me. I felt my face go hot.

'Just a minute,' said Jenko with a puzzled look. She got up and moved a bit closer to the screen. 'This photo, Ruby – where did you take it from?'

I couldn't think of a single thing to say. Everybody was looking at me. My face was already red from the joy of winning the competition, and now it was going redder still from the horror of Jenko's question.

'Up high,' I said, hoping that would be enough.

'But there are no hills at Fairfax Castle,' said Jenko suspiciously. She glared at me accusingly. 'Ruby, where were you *exactly* when you took this shot?'

There was no point in trying to invent a lie. What lie could I tell anyway? That I'd hitched a lift in a hot-air balloon? I took a deep breath and tried to make sure my voice didn't sound trembly or afraid. Instead, I tried to sound husky, like Will the Forester.

'I climbed a tree,' I said. Jenko's eyes flared and her face twisted into a vicious frown. Mrs

Wakefield looked alarmed and annoyed – I had ruined her photo competition, of course.

'Ruby! You were specifically told not, under any circumstances, to climb a tree! You could have had a serious accident! You could have been injured for life or even killed!' Jenko had gone quite white. I shrugged.

'It wasn't dangerous,' I said. 'I climb trees all the time.'

'You heard what Will said in his talk! That whenever the foresters climb, they always use hard hats and safety harnesses and ropes!'

I decided to say nothing. I just looked out of the

window. I saw a bird land on the supermarket roof. I wished I was up there with it.

There was an embarrassed pause. The teachers looked at each other.

'See me afterwards, Ruby,' said Mrs Wakefield menacingly. 'And under the circumstances, first prize will go to Hannah for her picture of the tower. Well done, Hannah!'

Everybody clapped while Hannah collected her prize: a book token. I clapped too – I just wanted to melt back into the class as soon as possible. But when the bell rang I'd have to be outside Mrs Wakefield's door. On the outside I was clapping Hannah and trying to look normal, as if I didn't care about anything. But on the inside I felt sick with dread.

CHAPTER 12

Who? What?
What do you mean?

'RUBY,' SAID Mrs Wakefield sadly, and shook her head. We were in her office now. I stood by her desk. My legs were shaking a bit. I was praying she wouldn't send a letter home about this. 'Why did you break the rules?'

I shrugged. 'I love climbing trees,' I said.

'Yes, but it's a highly dangerous thing to do.' She sounded irritated. 'You were specifically told not to climb the trees. Whatever possessed you?'

'I was on my own,' I said, 'and I heard men's

voices coming down the path. I was afraid they might kidnap me or something.'

Mrs Wakefield frowned. 'Why were you on your own? Didn't Mrs Jenkins tell you to stay in twos and threes?'

'Yes,' I replied coldly. 'But I get fed up of everybody, because all they ever talk about is boys.' Mrs Wakefield looked slightly embarrassed. 'I love trees better than people,' I went on. I was beginning to feel more confident now. I was determined to tell her everything so she would understand.

'I want to be a forester when I grow up.' I was almost surprised to hear this coming out of my mouth. It was as if part of my brain had made its mind up about things while I had been asleep. 'I want to be an environmentalist. I want to look after the forests where the monkeys live. I'm not interested in boys.'

Mrs Wakefield gave me a strange, wondering look. She played with her pen. She sighed again and shook her head.

'I'm glad you have a responsible attitude to the environment, Ruby,' she said, 'but you must not take risks or disobey the rules on school trips. We have the legal position to consider.' I was puzzled. Mrs Wakefield went on, 'If you had fallen out of

that tree and been injured or, God forbid, killed, it would have been the most tremendous tragedy. It would have ruined your parents' lives.'

In a brief flash I saw Mum and Dad weeping in the kitchen, getting through whole cartons of tissues.

'It would have cast a terrible shadow over life at the school for months, years, possibly for ever.'

I didn't argue. I didn't tell her I'd been climbing trees all my life. I didn't say that people have been climbing trees for thousands and thousands of years, and they'll go on doing it for ever – as long as there are people and trees. And what's more, I was going to go on doing it too.

I knew I mustn't say any of that. It's bad enough when I get into an argument with Yasmin. Arguing with the head teacher is totally pointless. You just can't win. I knew what I had to say.

'Sorry,' I said, though I wasn't. Mrs Wakefield looked pleased that I had apologised.

'Your photograph was very beautiful,' she said. 'Keep on photographing landscapes, but not from the tops of trees, OK?' I nodded. 'Run along now,' she said. 'And on Monday I want you to apologise to Mrs Jenkins for breaking the rules on her school trip.'

On the way home I suddenly had a thought. What would Will have thought if I'd fallen out of one of his trees and got injured or killed, when he'd told us specifically not to climb them? He would have been upset, obviously. He might even have blamed himself. He might have had a nervous breakdown. His life might have been ruined for ever. I felt terribly guilty about this, even though it hadn't happened. But I also felt a tiny little bit excited. I quite liked the thought of Will visiting my grave every day and sobbing his heart out.

When I got home I made an announcement.

'I'm going to be an environmentalist when I grow up,' I said huskily.

'A mentalist, more like,' sneered Joe.

At the weekend there was a barbecue to celebrate Yasmin's big sister Zerrin's birthday. Joe and I went, and a load of other people from Ashcroft School. It was in Yasmin's garden, which is huge. We sat under the trees and had the best time.

Holly arrived and came over to say hello. 'I'm going to be an environmentalist when I grow up,' I told her in a serious husky voice. 'Working in the forests to help save monkeys and orang-utans and things.'

'Oh, Ruby,' she laughed. 'Tell us something we *don't* know! You've been an environmentalist for years! I heard about your escapade on the school trip – climbing that enormous tree. For God's sake be careful and use ropes and a hard hat next time, you idiot!'

'I'm joining the Young Rangers,' I told her. My dad had promised that I could. Then I could do lots of things in the school hols and I'd probably see Will again and he could show us all how to look after trees.

'I heard about an old lady in Ireland who fell out of a tree in her nineties!' Holly grinned. 'That was you, Ruby Rogers, in a previous existence!'

She went off to get a hot dog from Joe, who was manning the barbecue. They started messing about and squirting each other with ketchup, and pretending it was blood, and laughing madly.

'I used to hope Holly and Joe would get together one day,' I told Yasmin sadly. 'But I've given up now. Now I'm thinking about the environment all the time, I can't be bothered with any of that love rubbish.'

'But, Ruby!' Yasmin giggled. 'They *are* together! Can't you tell? Look at their body language!'

I looked. To my eyes, Holly and Joe were just mucking about. But Yasmin could see something I couldn't. 'You're imagining things,' I told her.

'No!' she whispered. 'It's true. Zerrin told me!'

I stared at Holly and Joe in amazement. I could hardly believe it. They were an item! They'd got together all by themselves without any help from me!

'She might have told me,' I grumbled to Yasmin. 'It was a bit sneaky of Holly to get with my brother and not even mention it.' I felt a tiny bit jealous and left out.

'Oh no, Ruby!' explained Yas. 'That would have been *soooo* tacky! Holly's so stylish. It's way more cool for her just to never mention it and rely on you to pick up the signs. She knew you'd understand. It would almost be like a secret between you without ever mentioning it.'

I was amazed that Yasmin could understand all this and read people's body language and stuff. Thank God I'd got her to explain it to me. A moment ago I'd felt jealous and left out, but now I realised Holly and I were sharing a stylish secret.

'Anyway,' said Yasmin, 'you're not so high and mighty either. You say you can't be bothered with all that love rubbish, but I know you fancy somebody!'

'Who? What? What do you mean?' I spluttered, getting hot.

'You write like him, you talk like him, you wave your arms about like him!' said Yasmin, her eyes sparkling in glee. 'You've got a crush on that forester Will O'Hara!'

I blushed horribly, but in my heart of hearts I realised that Yasmin had understood something about me which I hadn't even realised myself.

'I so have *not*!' I said airily. I was amazed at her cleverness though. I would never admit I thought Will was handsome and wonderful, but in about ten years, if I met somebody my age who was a bit like him, who was also mad about trees and monkeys and stuff, well, I wouldn't rule it out.

I might just take ten minutes off saving the world and squirt ketchup at him at a barbecue.

Calling all tomboys!

Welcome to my world

In shops now

If you love trees and monkeys and you'd like to join my gang,
email me at ruby@suelimbbooks.co.uk to receive
gang updates and gangster goodies.

Catch you later!

Love,

Ruby x